TWIN TALES

JACQUELINE WILSON'S

TWIN TALES

TWIN TROUBLE
&
CONNIE and the WATER BABIES

Illustrated by
Catherine Vase

EGMONT

EGMONT

We bring stories to life

Twin Trouble first published in Great Britain 1994
Connie and the Water Babies first published in Great Britain 1996
by Egmont UK Limited
239 Kensington High Street
London W8 6SA
This edition published 2010

Text copyright © 1994 and 1996 Jacqueline Wilson
Illustrations copyright © 2006 Catherine Vase

The moral rights of the author and illustrator have been asserted

ISBN 978 1 4052 5460 1

1 3 5 7 9 10 8 6 4 2

A CIP catalogue record for this title is available from the British Library

Printed and bound in Great Britain by the CPI Group

Mixed Sources

Product group from well-managed
forests and other controlled sources
www.fsc.org Cert no. TT-COC-002332
© 1996 Forest Stewardship Council

FSC

Egmont is passionate about helping to preserve the world's remaining ancient forests.
We only use paper from legal and sustainable forest sources, so we know where every
single tree comes from that goes into every paper that makes up every book.

This book is made from paper certified by the Forestry Stewardship Council (FSC),
an organisation dedicated to promoting responsible management of forest resources.
For more information on the FSC, please visit **www.fsc.org**. To learn more about
Egmont's sustainable paper policy, please visit **www.egmont.co.uk/ethical**.

TWIN TROUBLE

Contents

1. Double Shock

'We've got something wonderful to tell you, Connie,' said Mum.

'You're going to be so thrilled,' said Dad.

Connie blinked at them both. Their faces were pink. Their eyes were shining. They weren't teasing.

'What? What, Mum? What, Dad? Tell me!' said Connie.

'Can't you guess?' said Mum.

'It's what we've always wanted,' said Dad.

Connie's heart started thumping inside her T-shirt.

'Oh, Mum! Oh, Dad! Are we going to Disneyland?' she said.

Mum and Dad blinked back at her.

'What?' said Mum. 'Oh, Connie, this is better than a trip to Disneyland.'

'Better than seeing Mickey Mouse?' said Connie, doubtfully.

'Mickey Mouse is only pretend. This is real,' said Dad.

'Am I getting a real mouse?' said Connie, perking up. 'Can I have a white one, please? And a black one too? And then they could maybe have babies, and they might come out in black and white stripes like very weeny zebras.'

'Do stop burbling, Connie,' said Dad. 'We're not talking about mice having babies. It's Mum.'

'Mum?' said Connie. 'Mum's having baby mice?'

'Oh, Connie,' said Mum. 'I'm having baby *babies*.'

'Baby babies?' said Connie. She didn't just sound doubtful now. She

 3

looked it too.

'Don't look so worried,' said
Mum, laughing. 'I'm not having lots
and lots. Just two. Twins.'

'Isn't it marvellous?' said Dad,
and he gave Connie a little nudge so
that she'd say yes.

Connie didn't say anything. She
was thinking. She wasn't sure she
liked babies very much. Connie's best
friend Karen had a baby sister called
Susie. Susie looked sweet enough, but
when Connie had picked her up to
give her a cuddle Susie had been sick
all down the front of Connie's best
teddy bear jumper. Connie had never

been very keen on Susie
after that. Come to think
of it, Karen wasn't very
keen on Susie either. She
screamed a lot. That was
just one baby. Two would
be twice as bad.

'Hey, Connie!' said Dad, giving
her another nudge. 'You know how
we've always longed for more
children.'

'Have we?' said Connie.

'That's why I had all that special
treatment at the doctor's,' said Mum.
'So I could give you a baby brother
or a baby sister, Connie. And now I

 5

can give you both all in one go.'

'It's going to get a bit crowded round here then,' said Connie. 'Where are they going to sleep, these twin babies?'

Mum and Dad looked at each other. Connie started to get suspicious.

'They're not going to come in with me, are they?' she said. 'There won't be room for three of us.'

'That's right,' said Dad. 'So Mum and I have had this really good idea.'

'What?' said Connie. She wasn't so sure about Mum and Dad and their ideas now.

'We thought we could make you a

special new big girl's bedroom,' said Mum. 'Then the twins could have your old room.'

'A new big girl's bedroom?' said Connie slowly. She thought about the extension at the back of her friend Karen's house. 'Ooh, are we going to build an extension?' she said hopefully, imagining a huge glass room jutting right out into the garden.

'Come off it, Connie, you know we couldn't afford it,' said Dad, and he sounded a bit grumpy. 'First it's Disneyland, then it's extensions. We're not made of money, you know. And when we're a family of five we'll have

 7

to be really careful with our money.'

Connie wasn't at all sure she
wanted them to be a family of five.
They'd managed beautifully in the
past being a family of three.

'We thought the junk room would
make you a lovely new big girl's
bedroom,' said Mum.

'The junk room!' shrieked Connie.
(She didn't actually say it. She
shrieked it.)

There were three rooms upstairs,
not counting the bathroom. There
was Mum and Dad's bedroom. There
was Connie's bedroom. And there was
the little junk room at the front of the

house. It was called the junk room because it was jammed up with junk; suitcases and an old broken sofa; cardboard boxes of books and an old bike; and heaps of toys that Connie didn't want to play with any more. Connie was starting to feel like one of the tired old teddies or droopy dolls. Mum and Dad seemed to have got fed up playing with her. They wanted a shiny new set of twins now. It was time to shove Connie in the junk room.

2. Name Games

Connie thought she might have to

balance her bed on top of all the junk

in the junk room and sleep crammed

against the ceiling. But Mum and

Dad sifted through all the junk and

threw a lot of it out. When the room

was bare they painted it deep blue

and stuck shiny stars up on the

ceiling. Mum made Connie a new

pink and blue patchwork quilt to go on her bed and Dad made shelves all the way up one wall for Connie's books and games and videos. By the time they were finished it certainly wasn't a junk room. It was a beautiful big girl's bedroom.

Connie couldn't help but be pleased, but she still didn't like seeing her old bedroom turned into a nursery for the twins. They didn't just have new paint and a new quilt and new shelves. They had new everything. Twin cots. Twin prams. Twin baby chairs. The twins weren't even here yet and already they seemed to be crowding Connie out.

Mum was getting big and tired and needed lots of rest. She couldn't dance to pop videos with Connie any more and sometimes when she was reading a bedtime story she nodded right off to sleep as she was speaking.

Dad was getting worried about money and kept doing sums on bits of paper and sighing. He didn't often feel like having a tickling match with Connie nowadays and didn't go swimming with her on Saturday mornings because he was working overtime.

'It's not any fun round here any more,' Connie said darkly. 'It's all because of those boring babies. Who wants to have twitty old twins anyway?'

'We do,' said Mum, firmly. 'Come and give me a cuddle, Connie.'

Mum was very big indeed now but Connie managed to squash into a corner of the sofa beside her.

'You'll like your baby brother and sister when they're here,' said Mum.

'Will I?' said Connie.

'And you're going to be a super

big sister and help Mum look after
the babies, aren't you, Connie?' said
Dad.

'Am I?' said Connie.

'What are we going to call these
twins, eh?' said Mum. 'Have you got
any good ideas, Connie?'

Connie had called the babies all
sorts of names to herself. They were
generally rather rude names. It
wasn't a good idea to announce these
to Mum and Dad, so she simply
shrugged.

'Come on, Connie, you choose,'
said Dad. 'Think of two names that
go together.'

'Mickey and Minnie,' said
Connie.

Mum and Dad didn't think a lot
of this suggestion.

'Chip and Dale? Laurel and
Hardy? Marks and Spencer?' said
Connie.

'Stop
being silly,
sausage,' said
Mum, tweaking
Connie's nose. 'How about two
names that go with your name?'

Connie thought hard. 'Bonnie
and Ronnie?' She thought this a
brilliant idea. She wasn't being silly

at all. But Mum and Dad were not keen. They decided on Claire and Charles. Connie thought these very boring names. But then she thought these were very boring babies.

Weeks and weeks went by and Connie was fed up waiting for the babies to arrive. But then one night Granny came to stay and Dad took Mum to the hospital. Dad didn't get back until breakfast and then he gave Connie a big hug, Granny a big hug and, when the postman knocked at the door, he very nearly gave him a big hug, too.

'It's twins!' he said, as if it was a

big surprise. 'A lovely little boy and a lovely little girl. Charles and Claire – a perfect pair!'

'I'm Connie alone. One on my own,' Connie muttered.

'What's that, Connie?' said Dad. 'You want to see your little brother and sister, eh? Granny will meet you after school and take you to the hospital.'

It was good fun at school showing off about the twins. Connie told Karen and all her friends; then she told the teacher and was allowed to write on the blackboard: CONNIE HAS A NEW BABY SISTER AND

 17

BROTHER. She did a picture of them too, with pink chalk and yellow for their curls. She wasn't sure what they looked like yet but all babies looked more or less the same, didn't they?

She got a shock when Granny took her to the hospital. There was Mum lying back in her bed, little again and looking very happy. There were two cots at the end of Mum's bed and there was a baby in each cot.

'Oh, aren't they sweet!' Granny cooed. 'Oh, what perfect little pets. The pretty little darlings!'

Connie didn't think the twins looked sweet or perfect or pretty. They were certainly little. Much smaller than she'd expected. Tiny weeny wizened little creatures. They didn't look a bit like Karen's baby sister Susie. They didn't even have any hair. Not one curl between them. They were as bald as Connie's grandpa – and much uglier.

'Aren't you lucky to have such a lovely baby brother and sister, Connie?' said Granny.

Connie didn't feel lucky at all.

3. Wailing Whimpers

It got worse when Mum and the twins
came home from the hospital.
Granny and Grandpa and all sorts of
aunties and assorted friends and
neighbours came crowding into the
house, too. They pushed past Connie,
barely giving her a nod. They rushed
over to the twins and then they
started gurgling and giggling and

goo-goo-gooing. (Not the twins. Granny and Grandpa and all the aunties and assorted friends and neighbours gurgled and giggled and goo-goo-gooed.)

The twins didn't respond. Sometimes they slept through all this attention. Most of the time they whimpered and wailed. For such tiny little creatures they could make an immensely loud noise.

'Hark at them exercising those little lungs,' said Granny, knitting busily.

She was knitting a tiny pink teddy bear jumper for Claire and a

 21

 tiny blue teddy
bear jumper for
Charles. She

didn't seem to have time to make a

new teddy bear jumper for Connie

even though Connie had explained

that her old teddy bear jumper had

never been the same since the mishap

with Karen's sister, Susie.

'I'd rather like a

pink teddy bear

jumper,' said

Connie. 'Or would

I like blue better?

I know! How about

pink and blue striped.

With a yellow teddy bear.'

'What's that, dear?' said Granny vaguely. 'I can't quite hear you.'

'Because the twins are making such a racket,' Connie said, sourly. 'They're giving me a headache.'

'It's just their way of saying hello,' said Granny.

'I wish they'd say bye-bye,' said Connie.

'Ooh dear,' said Granny, pulling a silly face. 'Someone's nose has been put out of joint by the twins. I think our Connie's gone a bit green-eyed.'

Granny often used odd expressions that Connie didn't

 23

understand. Connie went upstairs to the bathroom to give her face a quick check. When she came downstairs again Granny was still talking about her.

'It's just as well the twins have come along. Connie's a dear little girl but she can be a bit of a madam at times.'

'I suppose we have spoilt her rather,' said Dad. 'I've noticed just recently she's becoming very demanding. Always wanting this, wanting that. Trips to Disneyland. House extensions. We're not made of money. Especially now.'

'I hoped Connie would love the twins once they were born,' said Mum. 'I'm going to have to get her to help me more with feeding them and changing and bathing them. That way she'll feel more involved.'

'No, I won't,' Connie muttered. She sat down on the stairs and hunched up small, her head on her knees. It wasn't fair.

They'd all turned on her. They didn't like her any more, now they'd got the twins.

'Connie?' Mum called. 'Where are

you, dear? Connie, could you go and fetch me a clean bib from the airing cupboard, little Claire's dribbled all down hers.'

'Fetch it yourself,' Connie called, crossly.

She knew that would cause trouble. She decided she didn't care. Dad came out into the hall and hissed at her that she was showing them up in front of Granny (and Grandpa and the aunties and assorted friends and neighbours).

'I don't care,' Connie shouted.

Granny came out into the hall then.

'There! Didn't I say she could be a right little madam at times,' said Granny, shaking her head.

'I DON'T CARE!' Connie bawled, louder than both babies together.

It wasn't fair at all. When the babies got cross and cried they got cuddled and fed. When Connie got cross and cried she was given a good talking to and sent up to her bedroom.

Connie lay on her new pink and blue patchwork quilt and wept.

'Connie? Don't cry, pet.'

Mum came into the new

bedroom. She'd given one twin to
Dad to hold and the other twin to
Granny. Her arms were empty at
last. She could sit down beside
Connie and give her a cuddle after
all.

Connie lay snuffling
in Mum's arms, feeling
very much like a
baby herself.

'Want my
bockle,' she
said, pretending
to be a baby.

Mum laughed and pretended to
feed her. 'There you are, my little

baby,' she said. Then she sat Connie up straight. 'But you're not really a baby, are you, Connie? You're my big girl and you're going to be a good girl, aren't you? You're going to help me look after the twins? They need you to be their lovely big kind sister.'

Connie didn't feel one bit like a lovely big kind sister. Little Charles and Claire might very well need her. But Connie certainly didn't feel she needed *them*.

4. Blue Beads

Connie wasn't sure she wanted to be good. The twins were absolutely sure *they* didn't want to be good. They cried and cried and cried all that night. Mum and Dad were in and out of bed, feeding them and rocking them and changing them. The moment Mum and Dad stopped, the twins started. Most of the time they cried together. Every now and then Charles nodded off but Claire cried louder to make up for it. Then she screamed herself into submission and slept and Charles was startled awake by the silence. He cried. And then Claire woke up all over again and cried too.

Mum was nearly crying by the morning. And Dad. And Connie.

She couldn't find a clean blouse for school because the airing cupboard was chock-full of baby clothes. She couldn't get her hair to go right and Mum was too busy to fix it for her. Connie sighed heavily.

'Those babies kept me awake *all* night,' she complained. 'They kept crying.'

'Goodness. Did they?' said Dad, heavily sarcastic. 'Well, I *am* surprised.'

'Couldn't you feed them or something to keep them quiet?' said Connie.

'I feel as if I've fed five hundred babies,' said Mum.

She put her head down on the breakfast table and her eyelids drooped.

'You need some rest,' said Dad. 'Go back to bed, love. Connie and I

will hold the fort until Granny

comes.'

'But I'll be late for school,' said

Connie.

She didn't really mind being late

for school. It was arithmetic first

lesson and Miss Peters sometimes got

cross if you didn't catch on to things

straight away. But Connie felt like

being awkward. She really hadn't

slept very much last night and so she

felt very cross and cranky. Dad was

feeling cross and cranky too.

'Do you have to be so difficult, Connie?' he said, glaring at her.

'Yes,' said Connie, glaring back.

'Now, Connie,' said Mum wearily. 'I thought you were going to be a good girl and help us look after the twins?'

'*I* didn't want the twins to come barging into this family and spoiling everything,' said Connie. 'It's not fair. Why should I have to be good all the time? Why do I have to want the twins to be here?'

Charles and Claire started whimpering dismally in their

carry-cots, as if they could understand what she was saying.

'Oh dear, they've started again,' said Mum, getting to her feet.

'I'll see to them. You go to bed,' said Dad.

'You're not even listening to me,' said Connie.

'They probably just need changing. They can't need *another* feed,' said Mum.

'I'll take a look,' said Dad, unbuttoning both babies.

'Dad, you're not going to change them in the kitchen?' said Connie, pulling a face. 'Pooh! I'm trying to eat my breakfast.'

'And I'm trying to keep my patience!' said Dad. 'What's *up* with you, Connie? How can you be so rude and selfish? Why can't you help?'

Part of Connie badly wanted to help. She hated Mum and Dad being cross with her. But she was cross, too.

'Nobody asked me whether I wanted the twins. I'm part of this family, aren't I? And now it's all horrid and everyone's cross and you all keep getting on to me. You don't know what it's like for me. I wish there was some way I could make you understand,' Connie wailed.

Just then the doorbell went.

'It'll be Granny,' said Mum thankfully.

But it wasn't Granny. It was the District Nurse, come to check up on Mum and the babies.

'Hello there. I'm Nurse Meade,' she said, smiling.

Connie smiled back, suddenly not feeling so cross. Nurse Meade had a friendly face and a bright blue frock and her long black hair was twisted into dozens of little plaits fastened with tiny blue glass beads.

'Oh, I do like your hair!' said Connie.

'Do you, sweetheart?' said Nurse Meade, bustling into the kitchen and nodding and smiling at Mum and Dad and the two bawling babies. 'Well, tell you what. While Dad carries on changing your new baby brother and sister and Mum pops back to bed I'll give you one little plait of your own, eh?'

She lifted Connie up on to the draining board and twiddled with her hair. It seemed to be only a few

seconds before Connie had her own

tiny twisted plait bobbing about her

ear. Nurse Meade even fastened it

with two of her own blue glass beads.

'There. Don't you look pretty

now,' said Nurse Meade, showing

Connie her reflection in the kettle.

'You watch out for those blue beads

now. They're magic.'

'Magic?' said Connie, laughing.

Who was Nurse Meade kidding?

'Magic,' said Nurse Meade, nodding her head vigorously, so that all the blue glass beads on the ends of her own plaits swung and sparkled in the sunlight.

6. New Grannies

Connie didn't think much of Nurse Meade's magic beads. She glanced over at the babies and twiddled one bead wistfully . . . but little Claire and little Charles carried right on crying in their cots.

Connie went off to school with Dad. She was very late and Miss Peters was cross which wasn't at all fair, because it really wasn't Connie's fault. At least Connie had managed to miss half the dreaded arithmetic lesson, but all the children had been told to get into pairs for a measuring and weighing project. Karen was always Connie's partner, but Connie hadn't been there and Karen had paired up with Angela Robinson. Connie couldn't stick Angela Robinson. She went to ballet and was always showing off all the different dances she could do.

When it was playtime Connie wanted to have a good long moan to Karen about the twins. Karen didn't seem too keen. She wanted to prance about in the playground with Angela.

'That's not fair,' said Connie. 'You're my friend, not Angela's.'

'Yes, well, I want to be Angela's

friend too,' said Karen, and she pointed her toes and did a sort of twiddly skip towards Angela.

Connie didn't point her toes and do the twiddly skip. She hunched up in a corner of the playground by herself. She twiddled the blue beads instead of her legs, but wish as she might, Karen and Angela didn't trip mid-twiddle and fall down on their bottoms.

'Magic!' Connie sighed. 'There's no such thing. I didn't *really* believe that Nurse Meade.'

When they went back into the classroom, Angela said in a very loud voice that she thought Connie's hair looked stupid with one silly plait sticking out like that. Karen said she agreed. Connie said nothing at all. She decided she wasn't Karen's friend any more. She didn't seem to be anyone's friend at the moment. Not even Mum and Dad and Granny.

'It's all because of those twins,' Connie brooded. 'They've made everything horrid. And they've made me horrid too, so that no one likes me any more.'

She felt very miserable indeed as she trailed across the playground at going home time. Karen usually came out with her, arm in arm, but Karen was busy arabesquing with Angela. Connie peered round for Granny. She hoped she wouldn't give her a little lecture about being naughty. She didn't *want* to be naughty. Granny didn't understand

 what it was like.

Connie pulled on her plait, twiddling the blue beads so agitatedly that they clinked together. There was a weird little blue spark at the corner of her eye. Connie blinked. Ah, there was Granny. No, wait a minute. There were two other women pushing in front of her. They were waving and smiling and calling.

'Hello, Connie, sweetheart!'

'Ah, don't you look pretty, pet! Here, would you like some chocolate, darling, I'm sure you're a bit peckish.'

'And we'll buy you an ice cream

from the van. A giant 99 with strawberry sauce.'

'We've got a surprise for you too, Connie! We've been

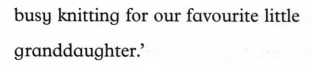

busy knitting for our favourite little granddaughter.'

Connie's mouth was wide open in wonder. So was Granny's.

'What . . .? Who . . .?' Granny stammered. Then she recovered a little, and barged between them. 'Now get this straight! Connie is

47

my granddaughter.'

'She's our granddaughter too, now.'

'That's right. We're her new twin grannies.'

They smiled twin grins and each took one of Connie's hands.

'But this is ridiculous! You can't possibly be Connie's grannies. She's only got one granny – and that's me!' Granny protested.

'You're her *old* granny.'

'We're her new twin grannies and we're much nicer, aren't we, Connie?'

The new twin grannies were remarkably like Connie's real granny.

They were the same height as Granny – but they were several stone lighter. They were wearing the same suit as Granny – but theirs looked much smarter. They had the same grey hair as Granny – but they had obviously just been to the hairdresser. They looked quite a lot younger than Granny, too.

Connie didn't know what to say. The twin grannies squeezed her hands, pulling her out of the playground and along the road. Connie's real granny had to trot along behind.

'You like us best, don't you,

Connie? Would you like a Mars Bar or a KitKat? No, I know, a Mars Bar and a KitKat.'

'Of course you like us best. How about a jumbo ice lolly after your ice cream?'

'Yes, please!' said Connie. 'I do like you both. Very much.'

There was a little wail from Connie's real granny as she puffed along the pavement, desperate to keep up.

'Can we slow down a bit?' said Connie. 'My other granny's getting left behind.'

'Good job, too. She's so bossy and bad-tempered.'

'Can't be bothered with you half the time. You don't want her.'

Connie's real granny gave a moan and stumbled, nearly falling.

'Granny!' said Connie. She stopped. She swung her arms and snatched her hands away from the new twin grannies. 'I like you. Well, I think I do. But I like my other granny, too. I like her just as much as you.'

'Oh, Connie!' said Granny and she straightened herself up and hugged Connie tight. They had a very long and loving hug. And when they looked up at last the new twin grannies had gone.

6. Purple Puddles

Granny bought Connie an ice cream
from the van on the way home from
school. A giant 99 with strawberry
sauce. She didn't mention a jumbo
lolly or a Mars Bar or a KitKat but
Connie knew she'd better not push
her luck.

'Thanks ever so, Granny,' she
said, licking happily.

'You'd better not tell your mum,' said Granny.

Connie and Granny looked at each other. Connie decided Granny didn't mean the ice cream. Granny glanced over her shoulder, checking that there was no one else around. Especially not another granny or two.

'Course I won't tell,' said Connie, slurping up strawberry sauce.

She felt quite a lot better. When they got home Connie called out a chirpy, 'Hi there, Mum,' the moment she got in the front door.

'Sh!' Mum hissed.

'Waaaaa!' wailed Charles.

'Waaaaa!' wailed Claire.

'Oh no,' said Mum. 'For goodness sake, Connie! I'd just spent the last twenty minutes rocking them, trying to get them to nod off. And now you've got them started all over again.'

'I only said hello,' said Connie, wounded. 'I didn't know the babies were asleep.'

'Well, they're certainly not asleep now,' Mum said grimly.

'I'll see to them, dear,' said Granny. 'Then I'd better get home to Grandpa. Connie, you go and put the kettle on, there's a darling. I'm sure

Mum could do with a cup of tea.'

Connie went into the kitchen and plugged in the kettle. She decided to be really helpful even though Mum hadn't been very welcoming. She laid the tray with cups and saucers and set out some biscuits from the tin. She nibbled a biscuit or two herself as she was feeling peckish, in spite of the giant 99 ice cream.

The twins were still yelling furiously in the other room. They sounded more than a bit peckish themselves.

Connie fixed herself a drink of blackcurrant juice. Karen's baby sister Susie loved blackcurrant juice. She'd glug so much she generally looked as if she was wearing purple lipstick. Maybe baby Charles and baby Claire might fancy a drink of juice?

Connie fished out two baby bottles from the sterilizing unit and filled them up with diluted blackcurrant juice. The bottles were a bit fiddly, and she had a job fixing on the rubber teats. Her fingers slipped, her hand shook . . . and suddenly there was a crash. The bottle didn't break but as it skidded across the kitchen floor it sprayed purple juice all over everything.

'What was that?' Mum called, and she came hurrying into the kitchen. She didn't look where she was going and stepped right into a purple puddle.

'What on earth . . .? Oh Connie!'

'I was just trying to help, Mum,' said Connie.

'Oh yes, this is a big help,' said Mum, crossly, getting the floor mop.

'Why were you playing around with the babies' bottles? I shall have to scrub them out and sterilize them all over again.'

'I thought they'd like a drink of blackcurrant juice, that's all,' said Connie.

'Oh, don't be so silly, Connie, they're far too little for that sort of drink. Why couldn't you just do as you were told?'

'You told me you wanted me to help you,' said Connie.

'Well, now I'm telling you to leave well alone,' said Mum, wringing out the sticky purple cloth and dabbing

 59

at the stains on her slippers.

'All right,' said Connie, and she flounced off upstairs.

It wasn't fair. She hadn't dropped the wretched bottle on purpose. She couldn't seem to do anything right. Mum didn't even seem to want to talk to her any more.

Connie flopped on to her bed, moodily picking at the patches on her quilt. She remembered she wasn't talking to Karen either. Karen and Angela had gone off together after school. She couldn't understand what Karen saw in that awful Angela.

'She looks really daft when she

dances,' Connie mumbled to herself.

She got up off the bed to do an imitation of Angela dancing, sticking out her feet and waggling her bottom rather a lot. She caught sight of herself in her mirror and giggled. She attempted several Angela-style leaps in the air, and landed with a thump.

There was a distant wail. And another.

'*Connie*!' Mum sounded very cross indeed. 'Whatever are you doing now? How dare you jump about like that! You've woken the twins *again*. Are you being deliberately naughty?'

'No!' said Connie, flinging herself

back on her bed.

She was in trouble again and it really wasn't fair. She wasn't being naughty. Mum didn't understand.

Connie buried her head in her pillow. She fiddled with her hair for comfort. Her fingers found her new little plait. She twiddled the two blue beads and they clinked together and even in the dark depths of her pillow

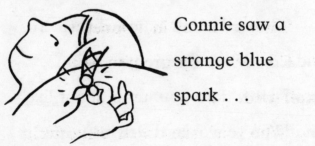 Connie saw a strange blue spark . . .

7. Fun Mums

There was a knock on Connie's
bedroom door. Two knocks. 'Are you in
there, Connie dear?'

'May we come in, poppet?'

Connie sat up straight. She
swallowed.

'Who is it?' she called, tentatively.

'It's Mum, darling.'

'Surely you know your own mum?'

Two twin mums stepped into
Connie's bedroom and smiled at her.
They looked a lot like her own old
mum, but these twins were much
more glittery and glossy. They were
both wearing Mum's sparkly sequined
evening dress and they were wearing
Mum's rings and bracelets and
necklaces all at once, so that they
jingled as they walked. They'd

sprayed on so much flowery scent that Connie sneezed.

'Do you like our perfume, darling?'

'Would you like a little squirt, mmm?'

They produced twin bottles and sprayed Connie's neck and wrists, while she wriggled and giggled.

'Connie?' It was Connie's own ordinary mum calling up the stairs. 'Connie, what are you up to now? What's that smell? You're not playing around with my birthday present perfume, are you?'

'No, Mum,' Connie called truthfully.

Mum wasn't convinced. She came plodding purposefully up the stairs.

'Connie, I'm getting very cross with you. You're telling me fibs, aren't you? The whole house *reeks* of perfume.'

She barged into Connie's bedroom and then stood stock-still in her stained slippers, staring at the new twin mothers.

'Who are you?' she gasped.

'We're Connie's new twin mums, of course.'

'Don't you ever knock when you come into our Connie's bedroom?'

'She's not your Connie.

She's mine!'

'Oh, you're only her old mum. She's got us now.'

'We're much much nicer, aren't we, Connie? Here, would you like to play Grown-up Ladies, sweetie? Try stepping out in my high heels.'

She kicked off her glittery dance shoes and Connie tried them on, staggering a few steps across her carpet.

'Those are my shoes!' said Mum. 'Take them off at once, Connie. I told you, you'll twist your ankle.'

'She's all gloom and doom, that old mum of yours, isn't she, Connie?

We're much more fun.'

'Would you like to
mess about with our
make-up, darling?
You'd look so cute
with a little lipstick
and eyeshadow.'

'Look, will you
stop this nonsense!' Mum shouted.
'You can't come bursting into my
house and taking over my daughter
like this. I'm Connie's mum and that's
my make-up and that's my best
evening dress you're wearing. And I
don't know how, but *you're* wearing it,
too. So both of you, take it off!'

'But it doesn't fit *you* any more, does it?'

'You've got *much* too fat.'

'*We* stick to our diet and fitness programme.'

'Cottage cheese and celery sticks and aerobics every day!'

'Am I going to have to eat cottage cheese and celery too?' said Connie, smearing blue eyeshadow on her lids and then blinking up at her new twin mums.

'Of course not, sweetheart. You're a growing girl. We'll cook you your favourite spaghetti bolognese every day, and you can have strawberry

 69

pavlova for pudding. Your old mum only gives you that on your birthday, doesn't she?'

'Look, I'm worn out and rushed off my feet at the moment. I haven't got time to cook,' said Mum, miserably.

'We *make* time. And we're much much much busier than you.'

'That's right. We go out to work. We have our own office and we earn lots of money.'

'So did I, once. But the twins are so little, they need me at home,' said Mum. 'And Connie needs me too, don't you, Connie?' She looked at

Connie rather
desperately.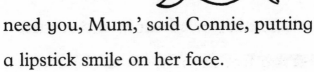

'Of course I
need you, Mum,' said Connie, putting
a lipstick smile on her face.

'But she needs us more. You can't
be in two places at once. We can. One
of us can go out to work and one of
us can stay home and chat to
Connie, easy peasy.'

'Those babies are bawling
downstairs. You'd better go and see
what they want now.'

The twin mums took hold of her
and turned her towards the door.

'But what does Connie want?'

said Mum, struggling.

'I want you, Mum,' said Connie, and she pushed past the two twin mums and pulled her own mum free of them.

They cuddled up close on Connie's bed and they didn't even notice the twin mothers sliding out of the door.

8. Best Friends

'I don't think I'm ever going to squeeze into this again,' said Mum, sighing. She'd found her own sparkly evening dress at the back of her wardrobe and was holding it up against herself. 'You might as well have it for dressing up, Connie,' said Mum, handing it to her.

'Oh, Mum! Really? Wow!' said

Connie, jumping up and down.

'And I'll find you some of my make-up – just the old bits and pieces, mind, not any of my good stuff – and we can make you up properly if you want. You look like a clown at the moment,' said Mum, rubbing at Connie's face with a tissue.

Connie pulled on Mum's frock over her T-shirt and perched on a chair while Mum started fussing around her, pretending to be a lady in a beauty salon.

'What colour eyeshadow would Madam like?' Mum asked, but as

Connie was choosing there was a cry from downstairs. Then another.

Mum looked at Connie. Connie looked at Mum.

'Well, they'll just have to cry for five minutes. We're busy,' said Mum.

She made up one of Connie's eyes very carefully, while the crying continued downstairs.

'It's okay, Mum. I'll do the other one,' said Connie. 'You'd better go and feed the twins again.'

'They're going to get as fat as elephants at this rate,' said Mum.

'They'll be growing trunks and trumpeting next. Sorry to interrupt the game, Connie. Here, tell you what – why don't you phone Karen and ask her to come round and play dressing up with you?'

'Oh yes,' said Connie. And then she remembered. 'Oh no,' she said instead.

'What's up?' said Mum.

'Karen and I aren't friends any more,' said Connie.

'Well, why don't you phone her up and make friends?' said Mum.

'I'm not sure she likes me any more. And anyway, she's probably

playing round at that awful Angela's,'
said Connie. 'She wants to be her
friend now.'

'Why can't you all be friends?'
said Mum.

Connie raised her newly painted
eyebrow expressively.

But she rang Karen all the same.
She felt shy and squirmy inside at
first, as if Karen was a stranger.

'Do you want to come round to
my house to play?' she blurted out.
She was worried Karen might say no
or make some excuse. But Karen
seemed quite happy about the idea,
thank goodness.

'Bring some dressing-up clothes and some of your mum's old make-up,' said Connie. She was about to hang up the phone. She hesitated. 'And you can bring Angela, too, if you really want.'

'She's gone off to her ballet class. She's a bit miffed with me, actually. I accidentally kicked her when I was copying one of those twiddly things she does with her leg stuck out, and she didn't half carry on about it. I think she takes all that dancing stuff far too seriously.'

Karen only lived ten minutes' walk away so she and Connie were soon playing dressing-up. They didn't take it seriously at all. They strutted around in long frocks and smiled silly smiles and shrieked with laughter at each other's antics. It didn't matter about making a noise because the twins were awake anyway, being fed and changed.

'Can I have a quick look at them?' asked Karen, when it was time for her to go home.

She'd already seen the twins when they came straight from the hospital and had privately agreed with Connie that they didn't look a patch on her baby sister Susie.

But now when Karen saw Claire and Charles, temporarily pink and peaceful in Mum's arms, she seemed impressed.

'Oh, don't they look sweet like that!' Karen whispered.

'Sweet?' Connie whispered back, staring at her baby brother and sister.

'You are lucky, Connie. I wish Susie had been twins,' said Karen. 'Look at them, they're as good as

gold. I thought you said they cried all
the time.'

'They do, don't they, Mum?' said
Connie.

'It certainly seems like it,' said
Mum. 'You're not good at all, are
you, twins? You're big bad babies who
bully us something rotten.'

Baby Claire and baby Charles
blinked blue eyes, all innocence.

Karen laughed and said goodbye.

'If you're late to school again
tomorrow I'll wait for you,' said

Karen. 'I won't be Angela's partner again. I've gone off her.'

'I was scared you might have gone off me,' said Connie. 'We are still best friends, aren't we, Karen?'

'You bet, bestest friends ever,' said Karen.

They linked little fingers and vowed that they would never break friends again.

9. Growly Bears

Dad was very late home. The car had broken down and he was in a bad mood because it was going to cost a lot of money to get it mended.

'Karen's dad's got a new car,' said Connie.

'Well, *your* dad's got to make do with a very very old car,' said Dad, bitterly.

'It would be nice to have a new car,' said Connie. She was simply making conversation but it seemed to irritate Dad.

'Well, we can't have a new car so there's no point asking,' said Dad, though Connie had done no such thing. Then he took a close look at her. 'What's all that muck on your face, Connie?'

'Make-up, Dad.'

'*Make-up*? Whatever's going on? You're much much too young to wear make-up!'

'It's just for dressing up, Dad. I wouldn't wear it out.'

'You go and give your face a wash this minute.'

'Oh, Dad. It looks lovely. I want to leave it on. And Karen's mum lets her wear pink lip gloss even when she goes out.'

'Connie.' Dad was starting to look very cross. 'I don't want to hear another word about Karen. Or Karen's mum. Or Karen's dad. Or any other member of Karen's family.'

'Karen's baby sister, Susie,' said Connie helpfully, because she was the only one Dad hadn't mentioned.

Dad didn't find this helpful. He seemed to think she was being

85

deliberately cheeky.

'That's enough,' he said, firmly. 'Go and wash your face at once. And then get ready for bed.'

'But it's not my bedtime yet!' said Connie, indignantly. 'Mum, it's not fair, Dad says I've got to go to bed and yet it's not my bedtime for another twenty minutes.'

'If you're not upstairs in *twenty seconds* then you will seriously regret it, young lady,' Dad bellowed.

His shouts seriously upset the twins, who both started bawling. Connie practically burst into tears herself. Her face was all screwed up

as she ran up the
stairs, and when
she was in the
bathroom a few tears spurted down
her cheeks. Blue tears, because of the
blue eyeshadow still on her eyelids.
The shiny blue tears made her
remember her two shiny blue beads.

'It's not fair,' Connie said,
sniffling. 'Dad can shout all he wants
and wake up the babies and he
doesn't get told off. And I've got into
trouble over nothing! I was being
good, for goodness sake. It wouldn't
be so bad if I was being bad, but I
wasn't!'

She twiddled the beads in her
little plait and they clinked together.
There was a blue flash
in the bathroom. Then
a knock at the door.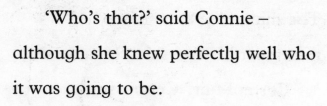
Two knocks.

'Who's that?' said Connie –
although she knew perfectly well who
it was going to be.

But there was no answer. The
knocking got louder. There was a sort
of scratching at the door. And then a
growl.

'What's that?' Connie called,
shivering.

'A great big ferocious growly bear

coming to hug you to death!'

'Two big ferocious growly bears coming to gobble up their little girl!'

The bathroom door burst open and Connie squealed as twin dads rushed into the room, growling and grunting.

'Grrrr!'

'Grrrr!'

'Help! Don't! Oooh! Tee-heeeee!' Connie screamed, as they picked her up in their pretend paws and tickled her with their pretend claws.

'Connie? What's the matter? Why are you screaming? Hang on, Dad's coming!' Dad shouted from downstairs.

He came running into the bathroom and bumped right into the twin dads and Connie.

'Get off my daughter!' Dad yelled, and he tried to drag Connie free.

'She's our daughter, too!'

'We're having a game. Connie loves a romp, don't you, darling?'

'You haven't played with Connie for ages.'

'You just get cross with her when

the poor kid hasn't even done anything.'

'I don't know what you two creeps are playing at, but *I'm* Connie's father!' Dad shouted.

'We're playing growly bears, eh, Connie? Grrrr!'

'And you call yourself a father, when you're no fun at all. Grrrr!'

'Will you stop this! Get away from my Connie. Get out of this bathroom, do you hear?' Dad bellowed, and he tried to push them out.

It was a mistake. The twin dads were quite a bit bigger and they had

 91

much broader shoulders.

'Who are you shoving, eh?'

'Getting all hot and bothered! You
need to cool down a bit.'

They picked Dad up and tipped
him in the bath.

'I'll hold him down while you turn
on the tap!'

'He could do with a swim!'

'Don't. *Really*,' said Connie.

'I don't know why you're sticking
up for him. He never sticks up for you.'

'And he hasn't taken you for a
proper swim for ages, has he?'

'It's not Dad's fault,' said Connie.
She couldn't bear to see Dad stuck in

the bath like that. 'Here, Dad. I'll help you out,' she said, and she took hold of his hands and pulled with all her might.

Dad shot upwards so rapidly that Connie fell backwards, bowling the twin dads over.

'Connie? Are you all right?' Dad asked, picking her up and hugging her even harder than a big ferocious growly bear.

The twin dads went on bowling right out of the bathroom, down the stairs, out of the door, out of sight.

 93

10. Baby Blue-Eyes

Dad tucked Connie up in bed that
night. He pretended she was still little
and tucked all her old dolls and her
big battered teddy in with her. He
made the dolls talk in silly little
twittery voices and he made the teddy
growl. The growling made both of
them look up and check the door, just
to make sure no one else was coming

to join in the game.

'It's just us, Dad,' said Connie. 'And Mum downstairs.'

'And the babies,' said Dad.

'Yep. The twins,' said Connie.

'I suppose it's been very weird for you, Connie. I bet it must have seemed like the twins were taking over at times,' said Dad.

'Mmm,' said Connie.

'I think it'll take a while before we all get used to being a family of five. We're all tired out at the moment because the little blighters keep us awake half the night, but once they get a bit older it should get easier. If more expensive,' said Dad, sighing a little.

'Poor Dad. It's not fair you've got to work more.'

'Oh, I'll manage. Though I do miss our Saturday morning swim. Tell you what, Connie. How about if we go swimming on Sunday mornings instead? Just you and me. Would you like that?'

'You bet,' said Connie.

'Night night then, poppet,' said Dad.

Mum tiptoed in from the twins' room to say goodnight, too. She sat on one side of Connie's bed, and Dad sat on the other. They had a grand family cuddle, just like they had in the old days. Before the twins.

Perhaps Charles and Claire felt left out. There was a little snorty sound. A snuffle. And then two plaintive cries.

'Oh-oh,' said Mum.

'Oh-oh,' said Dad.

'Oh-oh,' said Connie.

They all laughed, and then Mum and Dad went off to deal with a twin each and Connie curled up and went to sleep. She'd forgotten to undo the little plait. As she turned this way and that the beads bumped her head and

stuck in uncomfortably. Connie
mumbled in her sleep and fiddled
with her plait. One blue bead slid off.
Then the other. The plait unravelled
and the two beads rolled across the
pillow, off the bed, over the rug and
disappeared down a crack in the
floorboards.

Connie woke
up early the next morning. She could
hear an occasional car going by in

the road outside. She could hear a
few sparrows singing in the garden.
She could hear the hum of a milk
float. She could hear Dad snoring in
the room further down the landing.
She could hear Mum sigh sleepily as
she turned over in bed. But she
couldn't hear anything else.

She couldn't hear the twins.
They'd both been roaring their heads
off long before this, yesterday. Connie
waited. Still no sound. Not a wail, not
a whimper. She sat up in bed and
scratched her head. Her fingers
slipped through her hair. She realised
the plait had gone, and the two blue

beads. The beads had proved very magical indeed, after all.

Connie remembered what she had half wished when Nurse Meade first gave her the beads . . . She wondered if she might accidentally have clinked them together in the night. Maybe the beads could really take away twins as well as adding them?

Connie shot out of bed and ran into the twins' room. She charged to their cots, feeling sick with terror. Just for a moment she couldn't spot the two small heads on their pillows. But then she blinked and the teary blur went and she saw Claire in one cot,

Charles in the other.

Connie skidded to a halt, breathing a huge sigh of relief. It only made a little whistling sound in the room but it was enough to waken one of the babies. Claire. She made a tiny yowling sound like a kitten and opened her eyes. They were big and blue, almost as blue as the beads. They seemed to be looking right up at Connie.

'Hello, little sister,' Connie whispered.

Charles woke up, too. He did it differently, screwing up his face and smacking his small lips together before opening his eyes. They were big and bead-blue, too, and they blinked when Connie bent over him.

'Hello, little brother,' Connie whispered.

She waited for them to start crying. But they seemed surprisingly content to lie on their backs and look at her. Connie looked back at them.

'Maybe you're not so bad after all, little babies,' said Connie.

She stood between the cots, letting her hands dangle. She gently stroked their poor little bald heads. She felt very soft down. Maybe they'd soon get to be curly after all. She

 touched
their tiny
button
noses and
tickled

them under their chins. They didn't
laugh but they looked as if they
wanted to, if they only knew how.
Then she played with their small
starfish hands. Claire gripped her
tightly round the left little finger.
Charles clung to her right little finger,
his fist clenched.

'Make friends?' said Connie.

103

Contents

1. Swim Scare

'We're going swimming!' Connie sang happily.

'Sh!' said Dad. 'You'll wake the babies.'

Connie clamped her hand over her mouth, giggling. She certainly didn't want to wake her little brother and sister. They were called Claire and Charles and they were twins.

They were both bald, with beady blue
eyes, big tummies and bendy legs.
Connie's gran said they were the
most beautiful babies in the whole
world. Connie thought Gran had
gone a bit crackers. The twins looked
terrible.

Their behaviour wasn't up to
much either. They cried a lot during
the day. They cried a lot during the
night, too.

'Little monsters,' said Dad,
yawning. 'They just wouldn't stop

crying last night.'

'Tut, tut,' said Connie, shaking her head at the silly twins. '*They* won't be able to go swimming for years and years, will they, Dad?'

It seemed like years and years since Connie and Dad had gone swimming. Dad had been promising to take her for ages. But since the twins were born he was always too tired.

'*Next* Sunday,' he always said.

But now *this* Sunday he was really taking her.

'I love love love going swimming,' said Connie.

She made impressive sweeping movements with her arms, swimming through thin air.

'Look, Dad! I can remember how to do it,' said Connie.

She 'swam' right out of the house, tiptoeing down the stairs and along the hall. Dad closed the front door very gently behind them.

He put his ear to the door and listened. 'Silence! The twins are still asleep. And so is Mum. Lucky Mum.'

'Lucky *us*,' said Connie. 'We're going swimming.'

'Lucky us,' said Dad – but he didn't sound as if he meant it.

Connie practised her swimming strokes in the back of the car.

'Hey, stop kicking my seat!' said Dad.

'I'm doing my leg movements,' said Connie. 'Like a little frog. Just the way you showed me, Dad. I'm going to swim right up and down the little pool, you just wait and see.'

'Without keeping one foot on the bottom all the time?' said Dad, grinning.

'Cheek!' said Connie.

She got changed quickly in the cubicle at the swimming-bath. Her swimming costume was getting a bit  small for her. Connie had to pull it down hard to make sure it covered her bottom properly. It had a blue dolphin on the front, with a big smiley mouth. Connie gave him a little pat, her own mouth big and smiley.

'I'm ready, Dad! Let's get in the little pool quick,' said Connie.

But Connie and Dad found that the learner pool was roped off. There

were lots of mums and a few dads
and a lot of babies in the pool so
Connie ducked under the rope ready
to join them.

'No, dear, you can't come in
here,' said the attendant. 'There's a
parent-and-baby session taking
place.'

'But we always go in the little
pool,' said Connie. 'Dad's my parent.'

'She's my very big baby,' said
Dad, joking.

'Much *too* big, I'm afraid,' said
the attendant.

'Never mind, we'll go in the big
pool,' said Dad. He took hold of

Connie's hand. 'It'll be much more fun.'

Connie wasn't so sure. The big pool was very very big. The water got very deep and every fifteen minutes they switched the wave machine on. Huge waves rippled up and down the big pool and everyone shouted and screamed.

'The waves might knock me over, Dad,' said Connie.

'We'll keep to the edge when the wave machine is on,' said Dad. 'Come on, Connie. Let's get in the water, eh?'

Dad went down the steps into the

water. It came up to his waist. Connie went down the steps very slowly, one at a time. She would have stayed halfway down, but some bigger girls wanted to get in the water too.

'Move out of the way, you're blocking the steps,' they said, and when Connie didn't budge one of them pushed her.

It was only a little push, but Connie lost her grip on the handrail. She fell forward, screaming. She went splosh into the bright blue water. It closed over her head and she clawed and kicked in this new terrifying blue world. Then something grabbed hold of her. She was whirled upwards and her head burst out in the air, ears popping with the sudden noise.

'Poor old Connie! Were you trying to dive in?' said Dad.

Connie coughed and spluttered and clung to Dad. She put her arms tight round his neck and her legs tight round his waist, clinging to him like baby Charles or baby Claire.

'Hey! What's up? It's OK, you're not out of your depth here, Connie. This is the shallow end,' said Dad. 'Come on now, don't be such a baby.'

The girls who had pushed her were staring and giggling.

'Put your feet down on the bottom, Connie,' said Dad.

'I don't want to,' Connie said.

'Don't be silly now,' said Dad, and he pulled her legs down.

'No, no, don't, I'll go under!' said Connie, panicking.

'Of course you won't,' said Dad. 'There. See? You can stand up easily. Your whole head's out of the water.'

Connie stuck her chin up as high as it would go. The water lapped around her neck.

'I want to get out now,' said Connie.

'You've only just got in! I thought you were going to show me what a good swimmer you are.'

'I've changed my mind,' said Connie.

'Well, let's try one or two strokes, eh?' said Dad. 'I'll hold you up, don't worry. I'll put my hand under your chin, OK? I've got you. Just relax now.'

Connie didn't see how she could

possibly relax when her eyes were stinging, her ears were popping, her throat was hurting, her swimming costume was digging right into her, lots of girls were laughing at her, Dad was starting to get cross, and she was in a huge enormous pool of water and could drown any minute.

But she did try one feeble little kick, one pathetic sweep of her arms. And then there was an announcement and a shriek of excitement and suddenly the water started tugging and heaving as if it was alive, a great water monster ready to gobble Connie up. They'd switched the wave machine on.

'I'm getting out!' said Connie, and she fought her way to the steps.

Dad was cross because they'd only had five minutes in the water and it was a waste of money. Connie didn't care. She knew one thing. She was never ever ever going swimming again.

2. Spaghetti Worms

'Coming swimming on Sunday?' said Dad.

'No fear,' Connie said.

Dad looked at Mum. Mum looked at Dad. They both looked at Connie.

'Why don't you give it another try, love?' said Mum.

'I don't like swimming now. I hate it,' said Connie.

She stared at her plate. Mum had cooked spaghetti bolognese for tea, Connie's all-time favourite, for the first time since the twins were born. Mum hadn't had much time for proper cooking.

Claire and Charles had actually been very good for a while, cooing and kicking their legs. They'd started to get a bit niggly the moment Mum started serving up the spaghetti, but Dad had popped their dummies in place and they acted like stoppers.

Connie had been all set to enjoy her meal but now her tummy had gone tight at the very mention of swimming.

'I think it's time you learnt to swim properly,' said Dad. 'You were very *nearly* swimming before. Just a few lessons and you'll be bobbing about in the water, no bother.'

'I don't *want* to,' said Connie.

'I'll make sure you don't go under again, I promise,' said Dad.

'I know I'm not going to go under. Because I'm not going *in*,' said Connie.

She wound a portion of spaghetti round and round her fork. It was starting to look awfully like a lot of orange worms.

'Don't play with your food, darling. Eat it,' said Mum.

'I'm not very hungry any more,' said Connie, putting down her fork.

'For goodness sake, Connie,' said Dad. 'Mum's spent ages cooking you spag. bol. as a special treat. Now eat it up at once.'

Connie picked up her forkful of orange worms. She put them in her mouth. Just for a moment they tasted delicious. But then, as her teeth got working and she felt the forkful spread out over her tongue, she

thought she felt the worms going
wriggle wriggle wriggle.

Connie spat them out in terror.

'Connie!' Dad thundered.

'Connie!' Mum shouted.

Mum didn't often get cross but
she was very keen on table manners.
And she was very hurt because she'd
made the meal specially.

Connie tried to explain, but they
just thought she was being naughty.
It wasn't fair. Baby Charles and
baby Claire spat spoonfuls of food all
over the place every single mealtime
and no one ever turned a hair.
Connie pointed this true fact out to

her parents.

'Well, you're *not* a baby,' said
Mum. 'Even though you're acting like
one now.'

'And you're coming swimming
with me on Sundays whether you like
it or not,' said Dad.

'But it's so stupid if I don't want
to go,' said Connie, nearly in tears.
'You don't really want to go either,
Dad. Not early on Sunday mornings.
You'd much sooner have a lie-in.'

'I want you to learn how to swim.
It's very important. Every child has to
learn. And it's high time you did,'
said Dad.

'Why?' said Connie.

'Because you need to learn to swim so you won't ever drown,' said Dad.

'If I stay on dry land then I can't possibly drown,' said Connie. 'But if I go swimming then I could *easily* drown. I very nearly did last Sunday.'

'Don't be so silly, Connie. You just went under for a second, that's all. And I keep telling you, I won't let it happen again.'

'I know you've got a bit scared of swimming because of what happened last time,' said Mum. 'That's *why* we want you to go again. So you can see that there's truly nothing to be scared of. Swimming is great fun. Just give it one more try with Dad. OK?'

It wasn't at all OK with Connie, but she knew she was beaten.

Connie started shivering just at the smell of the swimming-baths. She was shaking so badly she could hardly wriggle into her tight swimming costume. The dolphin on the front was still smiling so she swatted him hard – and punched herself in her own tummy.

Connie had to be dragged to the big pool. Dad held her hand and did

his best to be very very patient with
her. He helped her down the steps
himself, letting her go very slowly.
When some other children clambered
round impatiently, Dad told them to
use the steps at the other side.

'You take your time, Connie,' he
said.

They were both shivering by the
time Connie
eventually got in
the water. And
then the wave
machine was
switched on, so
Dad hauled

Connie out of the water on to the side
and let her sit there until the waves
had stopped pounding up and down
the pool.

'Now, Connie,' said Dad, when
they switched the wave machine off at
last, 'we'll have a little swimming
lesson now. You're going to be a big
brave girl, right?'

Wrong. Connie tried, but the
moment the turquoise water started
lapping round her she couldn't be big
or brave. She squealed and shook and
shivered. Dad tried pulling her gently
along with one hand under her chin
and one hand under her tummy, but

Connie was so scared of the water she kept arching her back and rearing her head up.

Dad had to give up in the end. He tried sitting Connie on his back so that he could swim along with her.

'You can pretend I'm a great big whale if you like.'

This seemed quite a good idea. Connie clambered on to Dad's back

and held tight. Too tight. Dad swam several strokes and the water splashed right in Connie's face.

'Connie! Let go! You're pulling my *hair*!' Dad yelled. 'And get your other arm off my throat, you're strangling me!'

Dad put his feet on the ground. Connie slid off. Into the water. *Under* the water. In the terrifying blue world where she couldn't breathe.

Dad had her up and out of the water in a second, but it was no use. Connie was still crying when they got home.

3. Water Babies

'I'm not going swimming tomorrow,' Connie said on the next Saturday night.

'That's a pity,' said Mum. 'Because we are.'

'We?' said Connie.

'Yep. Claire and Charles and Dad and me,' said Mum.

Connie blinked.

'I think this parent-and-baby session sounds a good idea,' said Mum. 'I want to take the twins. But I can't dangle them in the water together. So I wondered if you'd help me out, Connie? We'll take the babies into the little pool – and Dad can go and have a good swim in the big pool. Yes?'

Connie wasn't sure.

'You like the little pool,' said Mum.

Connie wasn't even sure about that any more. And besides, she had a sneaking suspicion that once they were at the baths Dad would try to get her into the big pool after all.

'You promise I don't have to swim?' she said.

'Not if you don't want to. You just have to hold Claire or Charles in the little pool.'

'I don't think they'll like it,' said Connie.

'They love it in the bath,' said Mum.

Connie snorted. It wasn't as if the babies were super-brave. The least little thing startled them. When Dad played growly bears with them and went 'Grrrr!' they both burst into terrified tears.

'I always loved it when you played growly bears with me, Dad,' said Connie.

Mum bought the twins sweet little swimming costumes, red and navy stripes for Claire and green and navy stripes for Charles.

'Would you like a new swimming costume too, Connie?' said Mum. 'Your old dolphin one must be getting a bit small for you now.'

'I don't need a new swimming costume, seeing as I'm never ever going swimming.'

So she wriggled into her tight old

costume on Sunday morning. She had to help Mum get the twins undressed and into their new costumes. The swimming-baths had special red plastic changing tables. The twins liked to lie back, kicking their legs.

'They're practising their swimming strokes already,' said the attendant, smiling.

Connie couldn't smile back. The smell and the sound of the baths had made her go all shivery.

'You poor old thing,' said Mum, putting an arm round her. 'You're really frightened, aren't you?'

There were some girls getting changed nearby. They were listening. They nudged each other and grinned.

'Of course I'm not frightened,' said Connie fiercely. 'I just think swimming is an incredibly *boring* thing, that's all.'

It came out sounding much ruder than she meant. Mum sighed.

'Really, Connie! Do you have to talk to me in that sulky tone of voice all the time?'

Connie blushed and stuffed Claire's waving pink legs into her small swimming costume. Claire

started to whimper and moan
because she wanted to stay kicking,
stark naked.

'There! You don't want
to go swimming, either,
do you?' said Connie,
picking her up and
giving her a cuddle.

Charles started
crying too, getting a
bit fed up with all this dressing and
undressing. Both twins were still
yelling when Mum and Connie
carried them to the little pool.

'Perhaps this isn't such a good
idea after all!' said Mum.

The attendant looked at Connie. 'I thought we agreed before – you're far too big a baby!'

'She's acting as a sort of parent today,' said Mum.

'All right,' the attendant said reluctantly.

Connie held tight to baby Claire. Somehow even the little pool had started to look quite big.

'I don't think Claire wants to go in,' said Connie. 'She keeps crying.'

Charles was crying, too, but when Mum got in the pool and very gently lowered him so that the water lapped round his legs he stopped in mid-squawk. He kicked. He splashed. He smiled.

'Try Claire in the water,' said Mum. 'Charles thinks it's great fun.'

Connie held even tighter to Claire. She put out one foot, dipping the tip of her toe in the little pool.

'Come on,' said Mum. 'Charles, tell your sister that the water's lovely.'

Charles certainly seemed to think so. He wriggled determinedly, doing his best to get away from Mum. He waved his arms and legs in the water. He dipped his head and didn't seem

to mind a bit when he got wet. He
was smiling from ear to ear.

Claire was fidgeting and fussing,
obviously feeling she was missing out.

'Come in the pool, darling,' Mum
called.

But Connie couldn't.

In the end Mum had to fetch
Dad. He took baby Claire. Mum
looked after baby Charles. And
Connie sat shivering on the side.

4. Colouring Sharks

'You should see the twins in the pool. It's quite incredible!' said Mum.

'The little pets! They can really *swim*?' said Gran.

'Well . . . not properly, of course. But they bob up and down like ducklings,' said Mum.

'They must look so *sweet*,' said Gran.

143

'Even when they're in a really niggly mood and nothing else will comfort them, the moment they go in that little swimming-pool they start gurgling happily,' said Mum. She paused. 'Not like *some* people.'

Mum and Gran were talking very quietly, but Connie could still hear every word they were saying. She was drawing a picture of the twins swimming. It had started off a very good picture. Connie was clever at drawing. She drew Claire and Charles looking very cute in their stripy swimming costumes.

Mum and Gran had said it was a

beautiful picture. But then they'd sat
on the sofa together and went on and
on and on about the twins and
swimming.

Connie suddenly drew a great big

enormous
shark in the
swimming-
pool with the
twins. The
shark had a great big enormous
mouth glittering with sharp teeth. It
was swimming very near the twins. It
looked as if it was about to have a
delicious baby-snack for breakfast.

'Poor Connie! So this being

scared of swimming has developed into a real phobia?' said Gran.

Connie didn't know exactly what a phobia was, but it sounded feeble and pathetic and babyish. She *felt* feeble and pathetic and babyish. She bent her head over her drawing. There was suddenly a spot of real water puddling the swimming-pool picture.

'Connie?' said Mum. 'Are you all right?'

'Mmm,' said Connie.

'I've just been talking things over with Gran,' said Mum.

'That's right, dear,' said Gran.

'I've been telling your mum I'd love it if you came round to visit me on Sunday mornings. Would you like that, Connie? You can bring all your bits and pieces to play with – and maybe you'll draw me some lovely pictures to pin up in my kitchen. Let's see your picture of the twins swimming. Have you finished it?'

'Not quite,' said Connie quickly. She took her blue felt tip and scribbled hurriedly over the great big enormous shark.

'Connie, don't do it like that! You'll go over all the lines,' said Mum.

'I'm just colouring in the water,' said Connie.

The shark simply wouldn't go away, no matter how hard she coloured over him.

'Let's see,' said Gran, getting up.

'Whoops,' said Connie. 'Oh dear, yes, I've spoilt it.'

She tore the page out of her drawing book and crumpled it up in her fist.

'Oh, Connie!' said Gran. 'What a shame!'

'Never mind, Gran. I'll draw you another one next Sunday,' said Connie.

Next Sunday
she did draw
Gran a picture.
She drew herself,
on dry land.

'It's a lovely
picture, dear!' said Gran, and she
pinned it up on the kitchen wall.

Then Connie drew a picture of
Gran.

'Why have you drawn all those
dark bits on my forehead?' Gran said.
'I look as if I've got a dirty face.'

'That's all the wrinkles,' said
Connie.

'Oh dear,' said Gran, and

she sighed.

'Aren't you going to pin that picture up too?' said Connie.

'Yes, of course, dear,' said Gran, looking at her face in the shiny kettle, and sighing again. 'How about doing a portrait of Grandpa now?'

Grandpa wasn't very well. He spent a lot of his time having a little doze. He dozed all the time Connie was drawing his portrait. Connie went to show Gran the finished picture.

'I wish you hadn't drawn him with his mouth open,' said Gran, but she pinned that picture up too.

Connie wanted to watch
television now but Gran's set was very
old and kept twitching. Her video
recorder hadn't worked properly for
ages either.

'The hire firm is replacing them
on Monday,' said Gran, and her face
creased into a whole new set of
wrinkles.

'What's the matter, Gran?' said
Connie.

'Nothing, nothing. Tell you what
– you help me peel the vegetables for
lunch and then I'll read to you, eh?'

Connie wasn't too thrilled about
this idea. Gran had a whole shelf of

children's story-books but they were
all very long and old-fashioned. Gran
wasn't very good at reading aloud
either, not a patch on the people who
read on Connie's collection of story-
tapes. But Connie smiled and acted
pleased. She was trying to be good
for once because she was fed up with
Mum and Dad thinking her bad.

But Gran picked the worst
possible book. It was called *The Water
Babies*.

'I don't want that book!' said
Connie.

'It's a lovely book, dear, all about
this little boy Tom who's a chimney

sweep and then he becomes a water baby. Look, it's got beautiful pictures.'

Connie wouldn't look, Connie wouldn't listen. When Mum and Dad and the twins came to fetch her, Gran whispered to Mum that Connie had been a 'bit of a madam'.

Connie felt this was most unfair. She felt cross for the rest of Sunday. But she cheered up at school on Monday. She sat next to her best friend Karen. Karen had a baby sister called Susie, who screamed a lot. Karen drew a silly picture of Susie on the back of her school jotter.

 153

Connie and Karen got the giggles.

Connie was still smiling when she met up with Mum at the school gate.

'You look in a good mood for once,' said Mum. 'Come on, we're in a hurry. I've got to take the twins to be weighed at the baby clinic.'

'The baby clinic?' said Connie. 'Will Nurse Meade be there?'

'She should be,' said Mum.

'Great!' said Connie. 'She's *magic*.'

5. Giant Gerbil

'Hello, Nurse Meade! Remember me?' said Connie, running up to Nurse Meade.

'Of course I remember you, Connie,' Nurse Meade laughed, and all the little blue glass beads on the ends of her plaits twinkled.

'You've still got all your pretty plaits,' said Connie.

'With my special blue glass beads,' said Nurse Meade, and she winked at Connie.

Connie winked back. She wasn't very good at winking. She had to crease up half of her face in the process.

'Connie, are you making faces at Nurse Meade?' said Mum, shocked.

'She's just being friendly. We're special friends, Connie and me,' said Nurse Meade. 'How about helping me weigh your little brother and sister then, Connie? Off with their nappies and into the scales.'

They weighed Claire first. She

disgraced herself by doing a little wee in the scales. Mum got all embarrassed but Nurse Meade only laughed.

Then they weighed Charles. He wasn't going to let Claire outdo him. He did a little wee too. This time Nurse Meade had to dodge out of the way! She laughed even more. Connie laughed so much she had to clutch her sides and stagger.

'I'm going to wear my swimming costume next time I weigh these two,'

157

said Nurse Meade.

Connie stopped laughing. Nurse Meade looked thoughtful. Mum was busy mopping Claire and Charles and getting them dressed.

'Lots of people take their babies swimming now,' said Nurse Meade, cleaning her scales.

'Yes, I take Claire and Charles,' said Mum, trying to sound casual.

'And do they like it?' asked Nurse Meade, washing her hands.

'They love it,' said Mum. She glanced worriedly at Connie.

Nurse Meade was watching Connie carefully too.

'Do you like swimming, Connie?'
asked Nurse Meade.

'No. I hate it,' said Connie.

'Is that so?' said Nurse Meade.
'Hey, your hair's grown quite a bit
since I last saw you. Do you ever
wear it in little plaits like me?'

'They're too fiddly for me to fix
myself – and Mum's always too
busy,' said Connie. 'I loved it when
you gave me a little plait, Nurse
Meade.'

'Do you want me to give you just
one little plait now?' asked Nurse
Meade.

'Yes, please!'

 159

'With a couple of my blue glass beads to keep it in place?' asked Nurse Meade. She took two out of the pocket of her blue dress and held them up to the light. They sparkled a deep bright blue. A familiar frightening colour. Connie suddenly shivered.

'What's up, Connie? You loved my beads last time,' Nurse Meade said gently.

'Yes, but . . . they're swimming-pool blue. And I hate that colour now.' Connie hesitated. Nurse Meade started plaiting a lock of her hair. 'I'm a little bit scared of swimming, actually,' Connie mumbled.

'Is that so?' said Nurse Meade, still plaiting, as if it was no big deal at all. 'Ah well. We're all scared of something.'

'Dad gets cross with me. And Mum's ever so tactful but she really thinks I'm a baby. And Gran says I've got a phobia,' said Connie.

'I get the picture,' said Nurse Meade. 'Well, I wouldn't worry about it too much, Connie. I have a feeling things will somehow sort themselves out.' She finished the plait, holding it together with her finger and thumb. 'I can find a bit of ribbon for you if you really don't want to wear my blue beads.'

Nurse Meade looked at Connie. Connie looked back at Nurse Meade.

'A ribbon wouldn't be anywhere near as . . . magic,' said Nurse Meade.

'I'd like the blue beads after all, please,' said Connie.

Nurse Meade twisted them into place. Connie couldn't see them when she looked straight ahead but when she turned her head quickly she saw a little blue spark bob up over her ear.

Connie still didn't like being reminded
of swimming-pools – but the beads
were beautiful.

'I see Nurse Meade's given you
some of her beads again,' said Mum.

'Yes. They're magic,' said Connie,
very hopefully indeed.

'Were you talking about being
scared of swimming to Nurse
Meade?' said Mum on their way
home from the clinic.

'Mmm,' said Connie, not wanting
to talk about it now.

'I know you're very scared and it
must be horrible for you.' Mum
insisted on talking about it. 'I do

understand, darling. But you must see that there's really nothing to be scared of, not in the baby pool.'

'And boring old baby Charles and baby Claire bob up and down in it like little ducks. Why can't you all just shut up about it?'

Mum was now very cross indeed so when they got home Connie stomped off by herself into the back garden. She twiddled the two blue beads on her new plait. She was sick of Mum. She wished for two new twin mums. But the magic didn't seem to work this time. No new mums appeared though Connie looked all

around hopefully. She twiddled the
beads once more. 'Come on, you're
meant to be magic!'

'Who are you talking to?' said a
voice over the fence.

It was Gerald, the big boy next
door. He certainly wasn't magic, but
Connie liked him all the same.

'Come on, my little beauties,'
muttered Gerald.

'Who are you
talking to, Gerald?'
asked Connie.

'My gerbils
have had
babies. Want to

see them?'

'Oooh yes,' said Connie.

The baby gerbils were very cute
indeed. They were more like toddler
gerbils, bright-eyed and alert, with

fluffy coats and long
tickly tails.

'They're lovely,'
said Connie, enchanted. 'Let me hold
one, please.'

'Well, be careful. Don't drop it!'

'Of course I won't.' Connie held
her hands out over the fence and
Gerald gently dropped a soft little
baby gerbil into her palm.

'Oooh, it's so *sweet*!' Connie

whispered.

'You can have one if you promise to look after it properly,' said Gerald.

'I don't think my mum would let me. I don't think she likes gerbils. She's mad. They're the cutest little animals ever. But ever so tickly!' The gerbil was running up her arm and into the tunnel of her T-shirt sleeve. 'Hey, come back!' said Connie, giggling. 'Gerald, it's escaping!'

Gerald sighed. 'I told you to hold on to it. Wait a minute. I'll have to secure the others before I can help.'

Connie's gerbil was whizzing down her leg and was off up the lawn before she could stop it.

'Come back, little gerbil!'
Connie called, running.

The gerbil scampered
across the patio and in
through the open back door.
There was a sudden scream.
A very loud frantic s-c-r-e-a-m.

'That's Mum,' said Connie,
running harder.

Mum was in the kitchen, climbing
right up the cupboards, her head
nearly banging the ceiling. She was
yelling her head off.

The gerbil was on the tiled floor,
peering up at Mum. It didn't look

such a baby now. In fact it seemed
very big for an adult gerbil. It seemed
to be growing rapidly. It was a good
cat-size now, with huge pointed teeth
and an immense quivery tail.

'Run!' Mum shouted desperately
to Connie.

The gerbil heard the word 'run'
and decided to obey. It went charging
across the kitchen, its claws gouging
great tracks across the floor. It grew
at every stride. It skittered to a halt at
the kitchen unit. It could
almost get its huge head
over the edge.

'Aaaah!' Mum yelled

hysterically, hopping up and down.

'Calm down, Mum,' said Connie cheerily. 'I know you're very scared. It must be horrible for you. I do understand, honest. But you must see that there's really nothing to be scared of. It's only a little baby gerbil!'

As soon as Connie spoke the gerbil started shrinking.

'Come here, little gerbil,' said Connie, bending to pick it up. The gerbil shrivelled right back to its meek mild self, far smaller than Connie's hand.

'See?' said Connie, holding it up

to show Mum.

'Take it away,' Mum whispered hoarsely.

Connie did as she was told. Then she went back to the kitchen and helped Mum down from the cupboard. Mum was still shaking like a jelly.

'Nothing to be scared of now, Mum,' said Connie reassuringly.

'Oh, Connie! You were so *brave*,' said Mum. 'The bravest girl in all the world.'

6. Exploding Video

Gerald said the baby gerbil could be Connie's special pet, even though it would have to live in a cage in Gerald's back garden. She told everybody at school about George Gerbil.

It was art first lesson so Connie drew a portrait of George. She drew him looking rather big and fierce, almost filling up the entire sheet of paper. Then right at the top Connie drew Mum shrieking and climbing up the kitchen cupboards.

'That's very good, Connie,' said Miss Peters. 'But I think you've got the proportions all wrong. You've made your gerbil look much too big.'

'He did look as big as that, Miss Peters,' said Connie. 'Mum thought he did too!'

Connie wrote about George Gerbil in the English lesson and she chose gerbils as the animal for her nature project.

'You seem to have a one-track

mind today, Connie,' said Miss
Peters. 'Well, it's PE last lesson. I
suppose you're going to run as fast as
a gerbil, right?'

'Maybe,' said Connie, laughing.

She wasn't very good at running.
Or jumping or catching a ball. But it
didn't really matter, because Connie's
best friend Karen wasn't very good
either. They were generally partners
and puffed along together. Today
Connie and Karen were nearly last in
the race.

'Slowcoaches!' said Angela.
'Honestly, you two, you're hopeless.'

Angela had come first, even

beating the boys.

'Who wants to run like *you*?' said Connie.

Angela did ballet
and was always
sticking her feet out
sideways. Connie did a
funny imitation and
everyone laughed.

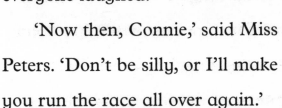

'Now then, Connie,' said Miss
Peters. 'Don't be silly, or I'll make
you run the race all over again.'

'Oh, Miss Peters! I hate running,'
said Connie.

'I know. Ah well, I don't suppose
you can be good at everything. And

maybe you'll come into your own next term.'

'What are we doing next term, Miss Peters?' Karen asked.

'It's a special treat,' said Miss Peters.

'Is it dancing?' Angela asked hopefully.

'Yuck! I hope not!' said Connie.

'No, it's not dancing. We're going to go swimming.'

'Swimming!' said everyone excitedly.

Everyone but Connie.

'Swimming!' she whispered, appalled.

'Yes, we've fixed it all up with the local swimming-pool. Our class can go once a week – in the big pool too!'

Connie closed her eyes. That terrible blue watery world seemed to be swirling all around her. What was she going to do now? Could she manage a terrible cold/stomach ache/headache every single swimming lesson? It might work once or twice, but Miss Peters was no fool.

'Oh help,' Connie mumbled.

'What's up, Connie?' said Karen.

'Nothing,' said Connie quickly.

'It's great about swimming, isn't it?' said Karen. 'Heaps better than boring old PE. You go swimming with your dad, don't you?'

'I . . . used to,' said Connie. 'We haven't gone much recently.'

Connie started to feel sick. She could see their whole class at the swimming-baths. Everyone showing off and teasing each other. She saw herself, shivering,

scared, screaming. She'd never ever ever be able to live it down.

She was still feeling sick when she

came out of school. Gran had come to meet Connie.

'Hello, dear. What's the matter? What's happened? You look dreadful, Connie!'

'It's nothing, Gran,' said Connie, hurrying to get away from all the other children.

Gran was in a hurry too, not wanting to miss her favourite quiz programme on television.

'Why don't you set your new video so that it records it while you're out?' said Connie.

'Oh, I . . . I didn't think of that,' said Gran, sounding odd. 'Come on, then, dear.' They were passing the ice-cream van. 'I think we can make time for an ice-cream,' said Gran. 'Would you like a giant ninety-nine with strawberry sauce?'

Normally Connie would say YES, PLEASE. But she was still feeling so sick about swimming that she simply shook her head.

Gran stared at her.

'Connie, there's something *really* the matter, isn't there?' Gran put her arm round Connie and held her close.

'Tell me what it is, darling,' said Gran.

Connie screwed up her face. Her

eyes were stinging and she was terribly scared she might cry. She took Gran's hand and hurried her down the street and round the corner. Then she blurted it out.

'Miss Peters said we've got to go swimming with the school next term,' she wailed.

Gran looked at her blankly.

'But that's good, isn't it, dear? You've got yourself in a silly state about going swimming with Mummy and Daddy. Now you can go with all your friends and learn properly.'

'Oh, Gran! You don't understand. I *can't* go swimming. I'm *scared*!'

 181

'But it's so silly to be scared, Connie,' said Gran, sighing. 'I don't know. I can't understand the way you children are brought up nowadays. Your mum shouldn't give in to you so. We just had to put up with things when we were kiddies. Nobody bothered to ask whether we were scared or not. We just had to do as we were told.'

Connie was extremely annoyed with Gran.

Gran hurried along the road. Connie trailed after her, twiddling the blue beads on her plait. As she went into Gran's house they gave a little blue spark.

Gran went into her living-room – and gave a shriek. Connie rushed in after her.

'Look!' said Gran, pointing with a shaking finger.

'Wow!' said Connie.

The new television and video recorder were hissing and buzzing and crackling ominously, lightning forks of electricity shooting off in all directions. They were covered with hundreds of knobs

and buttons, all of them lighting up
and flashing like Christmas-tree
lights. There were clocks and time

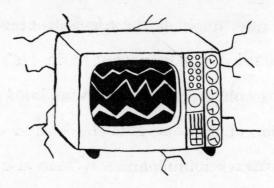

switches all over the place, numbers
blurring they were going so fast.
Different programmes danced across
the screen of the television set, while
the video recorder opened up all by
itself and sucked in Gran's favourite
video, The Sound of Music. It chewed
it all up in a split second and spat it

out again with a very rude electronic burp.

'Oh my goodness!' Gran wailed. 'I'll have to phone the television man again! I don't know what to do. He's shown me how to work it twice but I can't get the hang of it at all – and the instruction booklet is written in a completely foreign language. Grandpa's too old to work it out – and I'm so useless with modern machines. They scare me so.'

Gran cowered away from the television, squealing as an entire firework display shot out of the set and circled the ceiling.

'It's OK, Gran,' said Connie cheerily. 'It's a bit silly to be scared of a television, but never mind. I don't know. I can't understand the way you grown-ups feel about machines. We children don't act so daft. It's really easy-peasy. Look!'

She sauntered up to the television and video and pressed a button. They instantly subsided. Connie inserted *The Sound of Music* and pressed another button. It rewound, as good as new. Then Connie selected the right channel and pressed one more button. Gran's quiz programme came on to the screen.

'There we are, Gran. I'll set your video so that it records it automatically for you in future, OK?'

'Oh, Connie! You clever clever clever little girl,' said Gran, clapping her hands.

And Grandpa woke up at last and gave Connie a big smile.

7. Driller Dentist

Connie woke up with a start, her arms and legs flailing. She pushed back her duvet, gasping for air – and then sighed with relief. She was safe in her own dry bed – not down in the depths of that cold blue pool.

She glanced at her Little Mermaid alarm clock (oh dear, even that seemed sinister nowadays!) to see if it was time to get up.

'Mum! Dad! We've slept in,' Connie called, jumping out of bed.

Mum and Dad came staggering out of their bedroom, their eyes all peepy and their hair sticking up on end.

'Claire and Charles cried half the night!' Mum said. 'I had to give them another feed at four o'clock this morning – and *still* they didn't settle.'

The twins woke up at the sound of their names and started wailing.

'Oh no!' said Mum, staggering down to the kitchen to put the kettle on. 'Connie, you'd better share the bathroom with Dad. You have a very quick in-and-out bath while Dad shaves.'

'You haven't got enough water in that bath,' said Dad, his mouth all sideways because he was shaving.

'It's fine,' said Connie, having a quick swish.

'Don't be silly – it's only a couple of centimetres! You can't wash in that,' said Dad, reaching out to turn the bath taps back on.

'I don't want it any deeper!' Connie yelled.

'Oh, for goodness sake! You're not scared of the *bath* now, are you? This

is ridiculous, Connie. You're not a
baby. You've got to conquer this stupid
fear or you'll end up completely
loopy – and you'll drive us all daft as
well. Aaaaah!'

It was Dad who sounded daft,
screeching like that. He'd
concentrated too much on Connie
and not enough on his shaving.

Connie hunched up in her shallow
bath, twisting her little plait and
twiddling the blue beads for all she

was worth.

'What's going on? Are you all right?' said Mum, putting her head round the door.

'No, I'm not! I've cut myself,' said Dad, trying to staunch the wound with a little wad of toilet paper.

'Well, hurry up out the way and let Connie clean her teeth in the basin. I've just noticed a ring round the date on the calendar downstairs. Connie's got to go to the dentist for her check-up. It's a nine o'clock appointment – so you'll have to step on it. You can both have breakfast afterwards,' said Mum.

'What? What are you on about? *I* can't take Connie to the dentist. I've got to go to work.'

'I'm sorry, you'll just have to be late for work for once. I can't possibly take Connie in time.'

'But you know I can't . . .' said Dad, looking strange.

Mum sighed. 'Look, I'd normally take Connie, you know that. But she simply can't miss her appointment. Not like *some* people.' Mum sounded a bit strange too.

Dad still acted strange as he was driving Connie to the dentist. His hands were all shaky as he clutched

193

the wheel of the car,
as if he was very cold
– and yet he had little
beads of sweat on his
forehead. His face twitched every now
and then, and the little wad of toilet
paper stuck to his shaving cut
twitched too.

'Dad, are you all right?' said
Connie.

'Yes, of course I am,' said Dad.
But his voice was all high and wavery
– almost as if he was *scared*.

'You've still got toilet paper
stuck to your face, Dad,' said
Connie, as they drew up outside the

dental surgery.

Dad swatted it away from his chin. He switched off the ignition. He gave Connie a very weird wild smile.

'Off you go then, Connie. I'll just wait for you in the car,' he said.

Connie stared at Dad. 'But you have to come in too, Dad. You have to sign all the forms and stuff.'

'Oh dear. Right.'

He seemed to have great difficulty getting out of the car. He wavered all over the place going up the pathway to the surgery door.

'I think you might have really hurt yourself shaving. Maybe you've

 195

got tetanus or something, from the cut?'

'Don't be silly, Connie,' Dad murmured, and then he staggered into the surgery.

Connie followed him and looked round in astonishment. It seemed to have changed a great deal since she was last there six months ago. The waiting-room was terribly cold and all the pictures were missing from the walls. All the magazines and toys had been cleared away. There were just horrible leaflets with pictures of people with bleeding mouths and crumbling teeth.

Connie was great friends with the
pretty young receptionist – but she
didn't seem to be around today.
There was a fierce frowny woman in
her place in a crackly white uniform,
wearing a mask and rubber gloves.

She pointed straight at Dad.
'Aha! You're the man who's missed all
his appointments!'

'I'm sorry,' Dad said – and then a
terrible, achingly loud drilling sound
started up in the next room. It was so
ear-splitting that the wall vibrated
and Connie was jiggled up and down.
Dad threw himself to the floor,
his hands over his mouth, and

197

whimpered. Then the drill suddenly stopped and they heard footsteps outside.

Someone burst into the waiting-room, a huge terrifying white figure in cap and gown. He was holding huge steel pointed instruments in either hand and was chuckling manically behind his white mask.

Dad took one look at him and shrieked.

But Connie smiled. 'What's up,

Dad? You're not scared of the dentist, are you? This is ridiculous. You're not a baby. You've got to conquer this stupid fear or you'll end up completely loopy! There's nothing at all to be scared of.'

'Of course there's nothing to be scared of, Connie,' said the dentist – and he shrank back to his usual jolly self. His terrifying steel instruments vanished, happy music played in the prettily decorated waiting-room, and the young receptionist waved at Connie.

'Hi there, Connie. Are you here for your six-monthly examination?'

She looked at Dad, who was standing up sheepishly. 'Goodness! You've brought your dad with you today. It's a *very* long time since we've seen you. Would you like an appointment too?'

'I suppose so,' Dad said. 'I tell you what. I'll have my teeth examined if Connie stands beside me and holds my hand tight!'

8. Mermaid Magic

'Connie, your hair's getting to look like a little floor mop!' said Mum, ruffling Connie's unruly hair. 'I must wash it for you tonight.'

'Oh no, Mum!' said Connie, shaking her head vigorously.

Mum looked really worried. 'Oh, Connie – this being fussed about water is getting right out of hand.

You've *got* to have your hair washed, darling.'

'I'm not *scared*, Mum,' said Connie. 'I just don't want to lose my little plait with the blue glass beads.'

'Oh, the one Nurse Meade did for you. Yes, it does look cute. Well, I'll have a go at plaiting your hair after I've washed it, though I don't know how Nurse Meade twiddles those little beads into place.'

'They twiddle in a very special way, Mum,' said Connie. 'Let me keep my hair like this a bit longer, please!'

Mum got as far as fetching the

shampoo – but then Charles spat out
his dummy and started crying hard.
By the time both twins were fast
asleep Mum flopped into her
armchair and watched the television,
too tired to start shampooing. Connie
skipped off to bed that night with her
plait still in place, the blue beads
gently jingling.

She fingered her plait fondly as
she cuddled down to sleep – and
when she started dreaming she
chinked the two blue beads together
so that they sparked bright blue in
the dark of Connie's bedroom.

The blue seeped into Connie's

dreams. She found herself floundering in a vast pool of water. It was dragging her down, right underneath, and she was choking and struggling – but then someone caught hold of her round her waist and lifted her up and out of the water, her head bursting free into sudden sunlight. She wasn't in a pool at all, she was at a strange new seaside, with the blue waves sparkling in the sunlight.

Connie rose up out of the waves, through the waves, *on to* the waves, skimming along their surface as if she were riding a surfboard. The hands were still around her waist, holding her gently but firmly, steering her along, swooping her up on the crest of each wave, foam dancing about her ankles.

It was someone who looked surprisingly familiar, black beaded plaits flying in the breeze, all the glass beads as sparkling blue as the sea itself. This someone wasn't wearing a blue uniform. She wasn't wearing any sort of dress at all, and from her waist downwards she was all shimmering tail, flickering gracefully

as they leapt in and out of the water.

'You're a mermaid!' said Connie.

She looked down at her own legs again, wondering if she'd turned into a mermaid too. No, her two legs were still there, sometimes leaping right out of the water with neat pointed toes, other times kicking purposefully through the waves.

'I'm swimming!' said Connie.

The mermaid laughed, and a whole school of dolphins with smiley faces whistled and squeaked in a friendly way at Connie. They all skimmed the surface of the sea together and then dived downwards, disappearing.

'Oh, come back, little dolphins!' cried Connie. 'Where have you gone?'

She tried to peer through the water beneath her. She saw strange flowers and coral rocks and stripy fish and her new dolphin friends playing follow-my-leader.

'Can we go down there too?' Connie said.

The mermaid smiled again and then Connie found herself diving down through the water into a new brighter, bluer world and she could breathe easily and swim almost as fast as the dolphins and she chased

them all around
the sea garden
until she was tired,
and then she sat
on a rock with the
mermaid, who
combed
her hair with
a mother-of-pearl comb and then
plaited it and started to fix the two
blue beads back into place – but they
slipped from her fingers and spiralled
downwards through the blue sea,
down and down into the dark . . .

And then Connie woke up,
and it was light and morning.

She put her hands on to her hair. It was wet – as if she'd really been swimming in the sea. She felt for her plait, but it was just a little tangled lock, fast unravelling. The blue beads were gone.

Connie lay quietly, thinking about her dream. She thought about swimming. Somehow it didn't seem quite such a scary idea now.

She jumped out of bed and ran into her parents' room.

'Hey, Mum, Dad! It's Sunday. Are you going swimming with the twins?'

'I think I'll give it a miss today,'

Mum mumbled sleepily from under the duvet. 'They both woke up in the night and needed feeding. We're all too tired this morning.'

'I'm not a bit tired. And I'd like to go swimming. Will you take me, Dad? Please?'

'You want to go *swimming*, Connie?' said Dad, sitting bolt upright.

'Yes, please.'

'But . . .' said Dad. 'I thought . . .'

'Just take her!' Mum mumbled.

So Dad stumbled out of bed and took Connie swimming. Connie wasn't quite so sure this was a good idea when they went into the swimming-baths. She hesitated at the door, her lip trembling.

Dad didn't say anything at all – but he gave her a quick hug.

Connie knew he'd take her straight home if that was what she really wanted. But she wanted to swim. So she'd jolly well have to give it a go, even if she was scared after all. Very, very scared.

She stomped off into the ladies' changing-room, wishing like anything that she still had her blue beads to twiddle. And there right in front of her was a flash of blue! It was Nurse

 211

Meade, in a bright blue swimming costume to match her magic beads.

'Hey there, Connie!' she called.

'Nurse Meade!' said Connie. 'Oh, how super! Have you come for a swim?'

'I thought it seemed a good idea,' said Nurse Meade. 'So you've come for a swim too, Connie?'

'Yes. I thought it seemed a good idea too,' said Connie, hurriedly changing into her swimming costume.

The dolphin on the front was smiling all over his face.

'He's OK,' said Connie, tickling him under his chin. 'He knows how to swim.'

'I'll show you how to swim if you like, Connie,' said Nurse Meade, taking her hand.

They were out of the changing-rooms before Dad. The little learner pool was still being used for the babies.

'I guess it's the big pool,' said Connie, and she hung back a little.

'Getting in is the worst bit,' said Nurse Meade. 'Let's keep holding

hands as we go down the steps.'

They did just that – and somehow it wasn't quite so bad, even when the water was lapping right up around Connie's neck.

'I'll take you for a little swim shall I?' said Nurse Meade.

She held Connie gently but firmly round her waist and pulled her along through the water. Connie held her head up high and let her feet waft up off the bottom of the pool.

'Kick those feet a little,' said Nurse Meade.

Connie kicked.

'And paddle your hands through the water,' said Nurse Meade.

Connie paddled.

'There! You're swimming!'

'Only sort of,' Connie gasped.

The water washed over her chin and splashed her face but even that wasn't so bad now. Nurse Meade showed her how to dip her face right into the water and blow bubbles just like a little fish. Connie dipped and blew. Soon she dared bend her knees and duck right down. She didn't mind a bit. She wasn't scared any more!

Dad was sitting on the side of the pool, staring.

'Watch me, Dad,' Connie called. 'Let's do some more swimming, Nurse Meade.'

Nurse Meade pulled her carefully along while Connie paddled with her hands and kicked with her feet. Once the water splashed right up so that she spluttered, but she blew bubbles through it and went on paddling and kicking.

'Shall I let go just for a second?' said Nurse Meade.

Connie thought about it – and then nodded.

'Keep swimming, Connie,' said Nurse Meade, taking her hands away.

So Connie paddled and kicked as hard as she could – and for two whole strokes she was swimming all by herself. Then Nurse Meade clasped her round the waist again, keeping her safe.

'Well done, Connie!' she said.

'Well done, Connie!' said Dad, jumping into the water, absolutely thrilled.

'I can swim. I can really swim! Hey, let's go swimming every single Sunday, Dad, and then I'll be able to

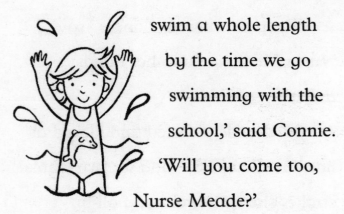 swim a whole length
by the time we go
swimming with the
school,' said Connie.
'Will you come too,
Nurse Meade?'

'Maybe once or twice,' said Nurse
Meade.

She smiled at Connie and Connie
smiled back. When they were getting
dressed after their swim, Nurse
Meade pulled on shiny green leggings
and pointy green pearlised boots. It
looked almost as if she had a real
mermaid's tail . . .